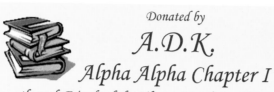

Teachers

A Level Three Reader

By Charnan Simon

Content Adviser: Kathy Rzany, M.A.,
Adjunct Professor, School of Education,
Dominican University, River Forest, Illinois

The
Child's
World®

Published by The Child's World®
P.O. Box 326
Chanhassen, MN 55317-0326
800-599-READ
www.childsworld.com

Photo Credits
© David Young-Wolff/PhotoEdit: 14
© Ernest Braun/Tony Stone: 13
© Frank Siteman/PhotoEdit: 9, 18
© Ian Shaw/Tony Stone: 5
© Jim Cummins/CORBIS: 6, 17
© Jose Luis Pelaaez/CORBIS: 3, 26
© Mugshots/CORBIS: cover
© Paul Barton/CORBIS: 10
© Peter Beck/CORBIS: 29
© Royalty-Free/CORBIS: 21, 22
© Ulf E. Wallin/The ImageBank: 25

Editorial Directions, Inc.: E. Russell Primm and Emily J. Dolbear, Editors;
Alice K. Flanagan, Photo Researcher

The Child's World®: Mary Berendes, Publishing Director

Library of Congress Cataloging-in-Publication Data
Simon, Charnan.
  Teachers / by Charnan Simon.
    p. cm. — (Wonder books)
"A level three reader."
Includes index.
Summary: A simple look at different kinds of teachers and the work that they do.
  ISBN 1-56766-488-1 (Library Bound : alk. paper)
  1. Teachers—Juvenile literature. [1. Teachers. 2. Occupations.] I. Title. II. Series: Wonder books (Chanhassen, Minn.)
  LB1775 .S544 2003
  371.1—dc21   2002151816

Have you ever taught somebody something? That's what teachers do!

Teachers are people who help us learn new things. Without teachers, we would have to learn everything by ourselves. A good teacher makes learning interesting and fun.

Two students watch their art teacher paint. →

Most teachers work in a classroom. The people they teach are called **students**. Some teachers work in classrooms with many students. Other teachers work with only a few students.

This student is learning to write. Her teacher writes new words on a **chalkboard**. She makes sure all the students are paying attention. She wants them to understand what she is teaching them.

This teacher writes on a chalkboard. →

Teachers use many tools to help them teach. They teach with books and videos. They use pictures, maps, and **bulletin boards**. Computers and the Internet help teachers and students find the information they need.

 A student and teacher work together on a computer.

Sometimes teachers take their students on a **field trip**. This teacher is helping his students learn about spiders. He is using the outdoors as his classroom.

Young students learn about spiders on a field trip. →

Gym teachers show students how to play games and do exercises. In nice weather, everyone likes to go outside for gym class!

A gym class plays outside.

This science teacher is in a classroom called a **laboratory**. He is teaching his students how to do special tests called **experiments**. What will this experiment teach them?

This science teacher carries out an experiment. →

Teachers often work after school. At home they plan what they will teach the next day. They correct tests and papers. They read books— lots of books!

People who want to be teachers study at a college or university. They have to pass special tests. They go to school for a long time before they can teach. They also have to practice teaching a class.

This woman is studying to be a teacher. →

Good teachers are smart. They are kind and friendly. The best teachers are always interested in learning more. Teachers are often active and work hard!

Not all teachers teach in schools. Music teachers often teach in their own homes. Swimming teachers teach at the swimming pool. Where else do you find teachers?

A music teacher plays the piano with her student. →

People like to learn new things all their lives. Even grown-ups need teachers sometimes. This exercise class looks like fun!

Teaching is a hard job. But it can be satisfying, too. People will always need teachers. Who is YOUR favorite teacher?

Teachers and students often learn together! →

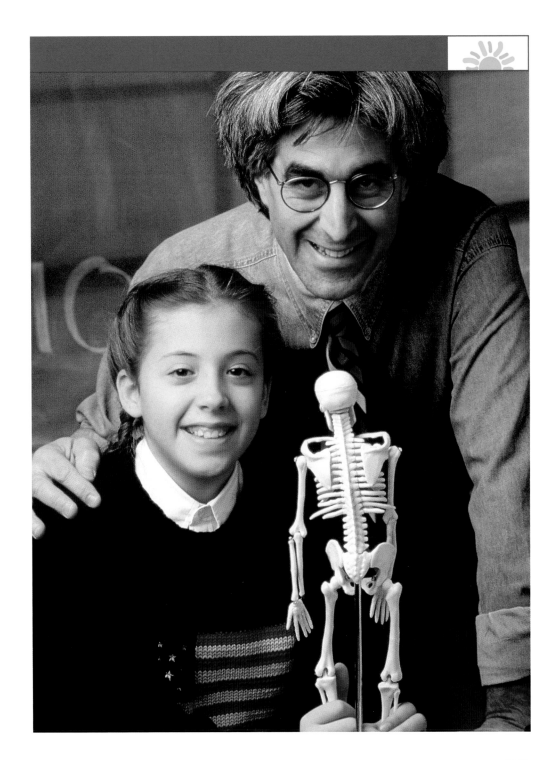

Glossary

bulletin boards (BUL-ih-tuhn BORDS)
Bulletin boards are boards that display information in a classroom.

chalkboard (CHAWK-bord)
A chalkboard is a flat, dark surface that teachers write on with chalk.

experiments (ek-SPER-uh-ments)
Experiments are special tests that help students learn more about science.

field trip (FEELD TRIP)
A field trip is a trip away from school to see and learn new things.

laboratory (LAB-ruh-tor-ee)
A laboratory, or lab, is a special place for studying science.

students (STOOD-ehnts)
Students are people who are taught by a teacher.

Index

To Find Out More

Books

Flanagan, Alice K. *Teachers.* Minneapolis: Compass Point Books, 2001.

Green, Carole. *Teachers Help Us Learn.* Chanhassen, Minn.: The Child's World, 1997.

Hayward, Linda. *A Day in a Life of a Teacher.* New York: DK Publishing, 2001.

Schomp, Virginia. *If You Were a Teacher.* Tarrytown, N.Y.: Benchmark Books, 2000.

Web Sites

Visit our homepage for lots of links about teachers:
http://www.childsworld.com/links.html

Note to Parents, Teachers, and Librarians:
We routinely verify our Web links to make sure they're safe, active sites—so encourage your readers to check them out!

Note to Parents and Educators

Welcome to Wonder Books®! These books provide text at three different levels for beginning readers to practice and strengthen their reading skills. Additionally, the use of nonfiction text provides readers the valuable opportunity to *read to learn*, not just to learn to read.

These leveled readers allow children to choose books at their level of reading confidence and performance. Nonfiction Level One books offer beginning readers simple language, word choice, and sentence structure as well as a word list. Nonfiction Level Two books feature slightly more difficult vocabulary, longer sentences, and longer total text. In the back of each Nonfiction Level Two book are an index and a list of books and Web sites for finding out more information. Nonfiction Level Three books continue to extend word choice and length of text. In the back of each Nonfiction Level Three book are a glossary, an index, and a list of books and Web sites for further research.

State and national standards in reading and language arts emphasize using nonfiction at all levels of reading development. Wonder Books® fill the historical void in nonfiction material for primary grade readers with the additional benefit of a leveled text.

About the Author

Charnan Simon lives in Madison, Wisconsin, with her husband and two daughters. She began her publishing career in the children's book division of Little, Brown and Company, and then became an editor of *Cricket Magazine*. Simon is currently a contributing editor for *Click Magazine* and an author with more than 40 books to her credit. When she is not busy writing, she enjoys reading, gardening, and spending time with her family.